Everything was about to change.

Evie Bear was moving home.

*For all the people who made the UK
feel like home for me, and the new friends
I've made in Los Angeles.*

First published 2018 by Walker Books Ltd
87 Vauxhall Walk, London SE11 5HJ

2 4 6 8 10 9 7 5 3 1

© 2018 Nicola O'Byrne

The right of Nicola O'Byrne to be identified as
author and illustrator of this work has been asserted by her
in accordance with the Copyright, Designs and Patents Act 1988

This book has been typeset in Intro Bold Alt

Printed in China

British Library Cataloguing in Publication Data:
a catalogue record for this book is available from the British Library

ISBN 978-1-4063-7425-4

www.walker.co.uk

Where's Home, Daddy Bear?

Nicola O'Byrne

WALKER BOOKS

AND SUBSIDIARIES

LONDON • BOSTON • SYDNEY • AUCKLAND

Evie Bear was hiding ...

she didn't want to go.

"I'll miss it, too," said Dad.

"We've made so many memories here."

"Why do we have to move?" asked Evie Bear.

"Well," said Dad, "everything changes eventually.
  And in the beginning change can feel sad.
  But it doesn't always. If nothing changed,
  there would be no more birthday parties."

  Dad helped Evie pack her books in the
  very last box and locked the front door
  for the very last time.
  Evie felt ... heavy.

"Goodbye, home," said Dad.

"Goodbye, home,"
  said Evie.

"Dad," asked Evie Bear, as Dad squeezed the last box in the truck. "How will I make new friends?"

"Hmm," said Dad. "Why don't you start with a smile? Those are the same everywhere."

As they set off, Dad had an idea. "I spy with my little eye,"
said Dad. "Something beginning with L."
"Leaf?" guessed Evie.

She already knew that leaves were Dad's favourite thing
to spy. Evie guessed "traffic light", "car" and "pigeons"
as the city began to fade away.

"Dad," asked Evie Bear, "what if I don't like the new home?"

Dad thought about this. "At first everything might seem different. But after a while you will notice all the things that are the same. And soon enough," said Dad, "you will find new things that you like."

Evie didn't reply. For a very long time, she looked out of the window. And then, in a small voice, she said, "This is the furthest from home I have ever been."

Evie Bear's tummy let out a long rumble and Dad had a very good idea ... blueberry pancakes – just like the ones they made at home.

"Where am I from now?" asked Evie Bear as they ate. "Our old home, or our new one?"

"Maybe a little bit of both," Dad answered. "We are all a mixture of the places we've been, the place we are now, and the places we're going to go."

Back on the road, Dad and Evie Bear drove for a long time.
Dad put on the radio and they both sang together loudly
as the sun began to set.

"We're almost at the campsite," announced Dad.
"We'll stop here tonight
and keep going
in the morning."

Dad tucked Evie Bear in,
but she couldn't sleep.
"Dad," said Evie.
"I'm not sure where
home is any more."

"I don't think home is a place,"
said Dad. "Home is more of a feeling.
Sometimes home is a cuddle.
Sometimes home is having the space
to be yourself. It can be all kinds
of things, but the best things about
home aren't things at all."

The next morning Evie Bear and Dad were up early.
Today they would reach their new home.

Tree after tree passed by before Evie asked,
"Dad, are we nearly there yet?"
Dad didn't reply.

"Dad," asked Evie, "are we lost?"

Dad scrunched up his big, furry brow.

"I know we're close," he said.

"We just need to find the river..."

"I have an idea," said Evie. "I spy with my little eye, something beginning with B..."

"Bird?" guessed Dad.

"I spy with my little eye, something beginning with T..." said Evie.

"Tree?" guessed Dad.

"I spy with my little eye, something beginning with ... R!" said Evie.

CB4 2JD

"RIVER! THE RIVER!" said Dad.
"There it is, Evie! You've found it!"

"Dad," asked Evie, "were you scared
when we were lost?"

"A little," said Dad, "but I wasn't
really lost with you beside me."

Dad unlocked the front door to their
new home. Evie Bear felt flitter-fluttery
butterflies in her tummy.
She felt ... excited.

"I think I know where home is," said Evie Bear,

as she helped Dad unpack her blanket and books.

"Home is people who love you. Home is me and you."

Then Dad read Evie Bear three bedtime stories and,

cuddled up in bed, surrounded by home ...

they both fell fast asleep.